About the Author

J. Anthony Vassell, better known as Julian Vassell, has enjoyed writing for as long as he can remember. Writing is where Julian always comes alive. His imagination and his desire to be different has him standing out from the rest in this matrix of creatives trying to break free.

J. Anthony Vassell

THE CURIOUS MR GAHDZOOKS
&
HIS CAUTIONARY TALES FOR
NAUGHTY CHILDREN

AUSTIN MACAULEY PUBLISHERS™
LONDON • CAMBRIDGE • NEW YORK • SHARJAH

A CIP catalogue record for this title is available from the British Library.

ISBN 9781787109964 (Paperback)
ISBN 9781786934581 (Hardback)
ISBN 9781787109971 (E-Book)
www.austinmacauley.com

First Published (2018)
Austin Macauley Publishers™ Ltd.
25 Canada Square
Canary Wharf
London
E14 5LQ

Dedication

I dedicate this book to Nehemiah Julian Kweku Vassell — my reason for working so hard, my reason for my continued fight for success, my reason for breathing every day.
To my first born, Nehemiah — this is for you.
Better days are coming.
Daddy.

Acknowledgements

My parents, Keith & Nolda Vassell, have been my mentors, my guides and two of my biggest fans from birth. Without their support and understanding throughout this journey, I'd not have had the mental strength or desire to put the words living in my imagination onto paper for the world to see and enjoy. Never will I forget what they've sacrificed for myself and my talented younger brother, Matthew Vassell.

Now, essentially, I wouldn't be here doing this today if it wasn't for the consistent pushing from my Rib, my partner in creative crime, my Wynsom. Not only does she love me for me (she really deserves an award), she's my loudest supporter, and all of this would still be a dream of mine if not for Wynsom continually being in my ears, telling me I can do it.

Her belief in me has elevated my confidence to be able to produce these tales.

Lastly, I want to acknowledge and thank Austin Macauley for believing in my words and allowing my words out, turning my dreams into a reality.

CONTENTS

INTRODUCTIONS

A long, long time ago
In a land far, far away.
A mischievous character lived,
He was real, or so they say.
By day he slept and dreamed.
Of all the mischief he would soon spill
At night he tip toed into bedrooms
Of his own valour and will.
When you sleep all calm and quiet,
Weary as the slumber washes over you
He stands in dark corners,
Pondering and wanders
About what he will do
Now I've got this far in and you are yet to know his name.
Tall and dark, a smile upon his face with a slim and slender frame.
His hat tilted to the side, with a cane in his hand primed and
ready to hook.
As your eyes open and the chill leaves the room, you hear him
whisper... Goodbye from **Mr Gahdzooks**.

He is not the stuff of nightmares
However, happiness is not his aim.
Naughty children are the ones to be careful,
Of **Mr Gahdzooks**' lessons and games.
He lists you all if you back chat
He notes it down if your veg is left untouched.
You didn't make your bed in the morning.
So at night your pillow you must clutch.
As through your open window.
Through the keyhole he can fit with ease.
Always say to people: thank you.
If you want something, end your request every time with 'please'.
If there is one thing, children, you should remember,
About the one we call **Mr Gahdzooks**
He feeds off mischievous children
If you're naughty, he loves it
So be good or it'll be you he will be coming to look.

Kitchen Manners

Mr Gahdzooks says…
Wash your plates
Rinse your glass
Knives and forks shouldn't go amiss.
Good morning! first thing
Good night! at bed time
To say these things your arm it should not have to twist.
They're manners, you know, they should be automatically firing…
Rat tat tat tat from your tongue.
Otherwise Mr Gahdzooks will be feeding off of all your wrongs.
'**Om nom nom nom.**'

To remind you daily about the life that you will soon see,
If you continue playing around at this **speed.**
In your dreams I will appear and when you awake,
I'm sure you will all **believe**.
These dreams, they somehow seem to actually be coming true,
Nightmares equally, they also are extremely real too.
You will have to think twice about the mischief
As I will inevitably find and ultimately sentence you.

Think more about the **consequences**
Think hard about your **deliverance**
Do you want me surprising you, taking you away from all
of your friends?
Take heed, young soul
Wrong doing is not your goal
Dirty plates in the sink should not be your end.

TRAPPED WIND

Prrrrraaaaaap prrrrrrrraaaaap; warm, funny air from your
mouth and also from below
You will be fine if you're excused, but if silence follows then it'll
be a decision you'll rue.
Mr Gahdzooks appears as you all knew he would,
You don't see him, children, if you're good.
Naughty children all **gassy** and **rude**,
Flatulence and gas leaves **Mr Gahdzooks** unamused.

He'll come and cork you up, you will bloat until you are blue
in the face,
There will be no trace.
As it's naughty children **Mr Gahdzooks** usually takes.
So save yourself the bother,
As your bum bum decides to **chitter** and **chatter**.

Always remember your pardons
Just remember to say 'excuse me',
Mr Gahdzooks will always have space for those children
that are naughty.

WASH YOUR GNASHERS

To the **left**, to the **left**,
To the **right**, to the **right**,
Put them together and everything will be all right.
Shiny and white, all glistening and clean,
Not a murmur in the house, it's all peaceful and serene.

He's weak, oh so very weak
Good children are no good
Mr Gahdzooks needs their energy
Secretly leaving sweets in places where parents had not put.
Luring them in,
With a mischievous grin,
If children won't misbehave, **Mr Gahdzooks** will find a way to win.
So with a rustle of the wrapper,
As the sugar coats their teeth,
He shows himself and appears from beneath.
If you brush and leave fresh,
Children, it is all for the best,
Sleep well in your beds, snore loud with clean minty breath.

All of Your Veg

There is nowhere to hide them,
Greens cannot be escaped.
The look on their face because of the strange foreign taste.
Mr Gahdzooks, his hands rub together in glee,
As you are too full to eat your runner beans.
Your plate should be empty, not a crumb or morsel left in sight.
If you have scraped your dinner in the bin, then you will have a
visitor in the night.
Mr Gahdzooks, his cunning and strength are seriously unmatched,
Greens fill his body with the insight to always find.
So if you lie
Do not cry,
Because all you had to do was eat your greens when
it is dinner time.

STRAIGHTEN YOUR BED

Crumpled and rumpled
Comfy and fluffy,
Soft and oh so very warm.
Mr Gahdzooks is awake,
Watching your mistakes,
In the bright and early new morn.

Did you make your bed or leave it unravelled and messy,
It's not the way to really start any day
Without straightening up your bed,
Where you peacefully lay your head.
He's sure you do know the correct and right way.
Mr Gahdzooks he lays still,
In waiting until,
You have corrected your morning routine.
He'll be on you if your bed looks a mess,
Heed this caution as **Mr Gahdzooks** is not a fan of the unclean.

You know all of his **ways**,
Yet you continue to **play**
Stop testing his patience as it will all soon fade.

So as your body ignites,
Please remember young star with all of your might.
Make your bed before you crack on with your new day.

REASSURING CONCLUSIONS

Mr Gahdzooks is not a bad person,
He merely does what needs to be done,
He does not want to be seen as one,
That arrives to destroy all of the fun.

He will only target bad behaviour,
Discipline the rude and those lacking manners.
"Give me…"
"I want…"
Are all ways to find yourself in **Mr Gahdzooks'** slammer.

As you have seen from the previous tales
Good children have nothing to fear.
No need to look under sheets,
Scared of what lies beneath,
There is no need if you have heard these tales loud and clear.

These are just warnings,
To children not wanting to abide to parents' rules and teachings,
To the ones not wanting to do as they have been told.
Avoid being **cheeky**,
No need to be **greedy**,
Make sure your teeth are **sparkly**,
Your bed is left presentable and **neatly**,
Greens secure inside your **belly**,
Please and Thank You come out **politely**.

If you pass gas, it's followed with 'excuse me',
With your behaviour, as good as gold.

Mr Gahdzooks will stay far
As long as you are all stars
He will remain vexed and fade away dying of hunger
Be good boys and girls for your parents and you won't hear of
Mr Gahdzooks any longer.